From Blind Faith to Open Heart

Mrigendra Bharti

Published by Sellbrochure Vymish Entertainment, 2024.

This is a work of fiction. Similarities to real people, places, or events are entirely coincidental.

FROM BLIND FAITH TO OPEN HEART

First edition. July 7, 2024.

ISBN: 979-8227572257

Written by Mrigendra Bharti.

Table of Contents

Preface: Echoes of a Shifting World

THE HUMAN SPIRIT CRAVES meaning, a guiding light in the vast unknown. Throughout history, we have sought answers in faith, weaving tapestries of belief that both unite and divide us. This story, "From Blind Faith to Open Heart," is an echo from a bygone era, a testament to the transformative power of questioning and the courage it takes to embrace understanding.

Within these pages, you will meet Yohan, a man whose unwavering faith finds itself challenged by a world clinging to tradition. His journey takes him from the comfort of his village to the opulent halls of a king's court, where whispers of tolerance threaten a long-established order. As Yohan navigates a web of deception and rigid dogma, he embarks on a personal quest that transcends religious boundaries.

This is not a tale of grand battles or mythical creatures, but rather a story woven with the threads of everyday life. It explores the complexities of faith, the yearning for acceptance, and the ripple effect that a single voice can have in a world yearning for change.

Prepare to be transported to a land where tradition and tolerance clash, where whispers of dissent become a roar for understanding. As you follow Yohan's journey, you may find yourself questioning your own beliefs and confronting the walls that may have unknowingly separated you from others.

This story is an invitation to open your heart, to see the beauty in the tapestry of faith, and to embrace the transformative power of understanding. It is a reminder that true faith isn't about blind acceptance, but about fostering dialogue and building bridges across divides.

So, turn the page and embark on this journey with Yohan. Let his story resonate within you, and may it inspire you to weave your own thread of understanding into the ever-evolving tapestry of our world.

Prologue: Whispers on the Wind

THE WIND, A RELENTLESS nomad, carried whispers across the sun-baked plains. It rustled the leaves of ancient banyan trees and danced with the dust devils swirling around the crumbling ruins of forgotten temples. These whispers spoke not of grand heroes or epic battles, but of a quieter revolution brewing in a distant kingdom.

Within the heart of that kingdom, nestled amidst towering palaces and bustling marketplaces, a seed of change had been sown. It began with a single voice, a young man named Yohan, who dared to question the rigid dogma that had choked the land for generations. His voice, at first barely audible above the chanting of priests and the pronouncements of a powerful king, gradually gained strength.

From village squares to palace halls, Yohan's message resonated with those weary of division and yearning for understanding. It spoke not of abandoning traditions, but of embracing a deeper truth – that faith, like the tapestry woven by skilled artisans, thrives on the inclusion of diverse threads.

This prologue serves as a window to the world Yohan will navigate. It is a world steeped in tradition, where faith is a sacred, yet stifling, force. It is a world poised on the precipice of change, where the whispers of tolerance threaten to upend the established order.

As you turn the page, prepare to be swept up in this unfolding story. Witness the challenges Yohan faces, the courage he displays, and the impact his unwavering conviction has on a kingdom clinging to the familiar. Remember, the most profound revolutions often begin with the quietest whispers, carried on the wind, waiting to reach receptive ears and ignite a spark of change.

About Sellbrochure Vymish Entertainment

Sellbrochure Vymish Entertainment, recognized as India's largest book publishing company, has made significant strides in ensuring its extensive collection of books reaches audiences across the global market. This rapid expansion is a testament to the company's dedication to disseminating knowledge and literature far beyond national borders. Central to its success is its affiliation with InkWhirl Media Networks, a reputable entity in the media and publication industry known for its innovative and strategic approaches. Within this network, InkWhirl Publication LLC operates as a vital division, further enhancing the company's capabilities and reach in the international market.

The visionary behind this enterprise is Mrigendra Bharti, the founder of Sellbrochure Vymish Entertainment. His foresight and passion for the literary world have been instrumental in steering the company towards remarkable growth and recognition. Under his leadership, Sellbrochure Vymish Entertainment has not only expanded its catalog but also established a strong presence in both domestic and international markets. Mrigendra Bharti's commitment to excellence and innovation has been a driving force in the company's journey, ensuring that it stays ahead of industry trends and meets the evolving needs of readers worldwide.

Sellbrochure Vymish Entertainment operates under the robust support of its parental organization, Mrigendra Bharti Group InfoTech. This affiliation provides the necessary resources and strategic guidance, enabling the publishing company to undertake ambitious projects and explore new markets. Mrigendra Bharti Group InfoTech's extensive experience in technology and information services has been a valuable asset, allowing Sellbrochure Vymish Entertainment to integrate advanced digital solutions in its operations, thereby enhancing its distribution capabilities and reader engagement.

Through relentless efforts and a commitment to quality, Sellbrochure Vymish Entertainment continues to break barriers and expand the reach of Indian literature globally. The company's diverse portfolio includes a wide range of genres, catering to different age groups and interests, thereby fostering a rich and inclusive reading culture. As it continues to innovate and grow, Sellbrochure Vymish Entertainment remains dedicated to its mission of making literature accessible to all, contributing significantly to the global literary landscape.

Connect With Mrigendra,
Thank you very much for choosing this book.
You can also connect with me on Instagram,
https://www.instagram.com/i_mrigendrabharti.official
With Love,
Mrigendra Bharti

Introduction: A Tapestry of Belief

THE HUMAN SPIRIT CRAVES a guiding light, a compass in the vast and uncharted sea of existence. Throughout history, we have sought solace and meaning in faith, weaving tapestries of belief that both unite and divide us. "From Blind Faith to Open Heart" is a story born from this very human yearning, a testament to the transformative power of questioning and the courage it takes to embrace understanding.

Within the pages of this book, you will encounter Yohan, a young man whose unwavering faith finds itself challenged by a world clinging to tradition. His life unfolds in a kingdom where rigid dogma reigns supreme, leaving little room for questioning or exploration of alternative perspectives. Yohan's journey begins within the familiar embrace of his village, a community steeped in the same beliefs that hold the kingdom in thrall. Yet, a seed of curiosity stirs within him, a yearning for a deeper understanding of the world beyond the confines of his upbringing.

This curiosity propels him towards a pivotal encounter – a meeting with Swami Vivekananda, a thought leader whose message of tolerance and open dialogue resonates deeply with Yohan. This encounter serves as a catalyst, shattering the comfortable illusion of a monolithic faith and exposing Yohan to the shimmering threads of diverse beliefs waiting to be woven into the tapestry of his understanding.

However, the path to embracing these new perspectives is fraught with challenges. The kingdom's power structure thrives on the rigidity of its doctrines. Yohan's newfound openness is met with suspicion and hostility, particularly from those threatened by the ripples of change his questioning might unleash. As Yohan embarks on a personal quest that transcends religious boundaries, he finds himself navigating a labyrinth of courtly intrigue, deception, and fierce resistance.

This is not a tale of grand battles or mythical creatures. Instead, it delves into the complexities of everyday life, exploring the internal struggles of faith, the yearning for acceptance, and the ripple effect that a single voice, raised in dissent, can have in a world desperately yearning for change.

Prepare to be transported to a world where tradition and tolerance clash, where whispers of rebellion become a roar for understanding. As you follow Yohan's journey, you may find yourself questioning your own beliefs and confronting the walls that may have unknowingly separated you from others.

This is an invitation to open your heart, to see the beauty in the tapestry of faith, and to embrace the transformative power of understanding. It is a reminder that true faith isn't about blind acceptance, but about fostering dialogue and building bridges across divides. So, turn the page and join Yohan on his quest. Let his story resonate within you, and may it inspire you to weave your own thread of understanding into the ever-evolving tapestry of our world.

Chapter 1: The Shadow of Doubt

The bustling city of Aayuthapura pulsed with vibrant life. Its narrow streets, a maze of colorful shops and aromatic food stalls, teemed with the daily rhythm of commerce and community. Nestled within this vibrant tapestry lived Yohan, a young man whose life was an ode to devotion. From the break of dawn, marked by the melodious chiming of the temple bells, to the gentle lull of the evening prayer, Yohan's days were meticulously woven with rituals and offerings dedicated to Shani Bhagwan Ji, the Lord of Karma and Justice.

Yohan's mornings began in the serene embrace of the local Shani temple. The air, heavy with the sweet fragrance of incense and the chanting of mantras, held a sense of calm that soothed his soul. He would meticulously perform the ablutions, the cool water washing away the sleep and anxieties from the previous day. Dressed in simple white dhoti and kurta, Yohan would then stand before the imposing black marble idol of Shani Bhagwan Ji. The deity, depicted with a stern gaze and a crow perched on his shoulder, embodied both justice and the inevitable consequences of one's actions. Yohan offered prayers, chanting hymns in a melodious tone honed by years of devotion. Each word carried a heartfelt plea for blessings and protection, a testament to his unwavering faith.

Leaving the temple with a newfound sense of peace, Yohan would traverse the bustling streets to his small, yet well-maintained shop. He ran a modest business selling handcrafted wooden artifacts, each piece a labor of love passed down from generations. His father, a skilled artisan, had instilled in him not just the art of woodworking but also the importance of honesty and fair trade. Yohan meticulously selected each piece for his shop, ensuring they were crafted with quality materials and displayed the intricate details that were the hallmark of his family's legacy. His customers, a mix of locals and tourists, appreciated his genuine dedication and fair pricing. Yohan wasn't driven by the sole pursuit of monetary gain; his primary concern was providing an honest service and earning a decent living through his craft.

The afternoon found Yohan engrossed in work, his nimble fingers expertly shaping the wood, transforming raw materials into exquisite artifacts. The rhythmic tapping of the hammer and the gentle rasp of sandpaper filled the air, a symphony of creation. During these quiet moments, Yohan would often hum hymns devoted to Shani Bhagwan Ji, his faith a constant companion. He believed in the deity's guiding hand, ensuring that his work would find appreciation and his business would flourish.

As the sun began its descent, painting the sky in hues of orange and red, Yohan would head back to the temple for the evening aarti. The rhythmic beating of the dhol and the clanging of cymbals filled the air, a vibrant melody that echoed through the streets. Devotees, mirroring Yohan's devotion, gathered to offer prayers and witness the ceremonial lighting of oil lamps before the idol. The warm glow illuminated the intricate details of the deity, a beacon of hope and justice amidst the bustling city. Yohan immersed himself in the chants and prayers, his heart brimming with a deep sense of reverence.

Returning home after the evening aarti, Yohan would sit with his family for a simple meal. His wife, Maya, a woman with gentle eyes and a kind smile, shared his unwavering faith in Shani Bhagwan Ji. Together, they would recount their day, their conversations peppered with references to deities and religious practices. Their evenings were often spent reading scriptures or watching devotional television programs, further strengthening their spiritual connection.

Before retiring to bed, Yohan would meticulously follow his nightly rituals. He diligently performed a puja at his home altar, offering flowers, incense, and sweets to his deities. As he recited verses from sacred texts, a sense of serenity washed over him. His days, meticulously woven with devotion and faith, were a testament to his unwavering belief in the divine. He felt secure in the knowledge that Shani Bhagwan Ji watched over him, ensuring his well-being and guiding his path. Little did Yohan know, the very foundation of his faith would soon be challenged, casting a long shadow of doubt over his previously unwavering devotion.

Yohan's life, a meticulously crafted routine of faith and dedication, continued for several years. His business thrived, attracting a loyal clientele who appreciated his craftsmanship and fair prices. Maya, his wife, remained a source of unwavering support, her gentle nature and shared faith a constant comfort. However, a subtle shift began to occur, a series of seemingly insignificant events that chipped away at the foundation of Yohan's unshakeable faith.

The first crack appeared in the form of a prolonged monsoon season. The incessant rains that had initially brought relief to the parched land turned into a relentless downpour. The streets turned muddy, and shops like Yohan's, located in a low-lying area, saw a significant drop in foot traffic. Days turned into weeks, and the rain continued to fall, forcing Yohan to dip into his savings to make ends meet. The worry lines etching themselves onto his forehead spoke volumes of the anxiety gnawing at his heart. He continued his daily rituals, his prayers now infused with a desperate plea for the rains to stop.

Days bled into weeks, and the unrelenting monsoon finally began to subside. However, by then, the damage was done. Tourists, weary of the weather, were opting for destinations with sunnier skies. Local customers, themselves facing financial difficulties, were hesitant to spend money on non-essential items. Yohan's usually bustling shop became shrouded in an unsettling silence, broken only by the relentless dripping of water leaking through the roof. His savings dwindled, and anxiety began to cloud his mind. His routine prayers, once an expression of unwavering faith, now carried a tinge of frustration and doubt.

Another blow came in the form of illness. Maya, usually the picture of health, began experiencing debilitating headaches and body aches. Their meager savings, further depleted by the monsoon, were stretched thin trying to afford medical care. The doctor, a kind yet stern man, diagnosed her with a chronic condition that required ongoing medication and frequent checkups. Despair settled upon Yohan like a heavy cloak. His faith, once a source of strength, began to feel inadequate in the face of these mounting challenges.

The whispers of doubt that had begun as a faint murmur grew louder. "Why is this happening to me?" he would ask himself in the quiet moments of contemplation. "I have always followed the righteous path, shown devotion to Shani Bhagwan Ji, yet my life seems to be spiraling out of control." He questioned whether his faith, his meticulous adherence to rituals, had been in vain. Was Shani Bhagwan Ji oblivious to his plight, or worse, indifferent?

These unsettling thoughts began to poison his once pure devotion. His prayers, once filled with heartfelt conviction, became tinged with a sense of desperation, almost bordering on accusation. He felt the warmth of his faith slipping away, replaced by a coldness that gnawed at his soul. The previously comforting rituals started to feel hollow, mere motions devoid of their previous meaning.

Yohan found himself drawn into conversations with fellow shopkeepers, men who scoffed at his unwavering faith. They spoke of life being a gamble, success a fickle mistress, and divine intervention a mere figment of wishful thinking. Their words, laced with cynicism, resonated with his current state of despair. Perhaps, he thought, they were right. Maybe faith was just a crutch, a way for those unable to control their destinies to find solace in an illusion.

As doubts festered in his mind, Yohan began to neglect his usual routines. He started missing his evening aartis at the temple, the once comforting chants now a source of irritation. The simple act of prayer felt an unwelcome burden, a reminder of his unfulfilled wishes and unanswered pleas. He saw other shopkeepers, those who scoffed at his faith, seemingly doing well. Their businesses remained open, seemingly blessed with good fortune that eluded him despite his unwavering devotion.

The once vibrant tapestry of his life, woven with faith and devotion, began to fray at the edges. The joy of his work had been replaced by a grinding sense of despair. His evenings, previously a time for shared faith and spiritual connection with Maya, were now filled with an unsettling silence. The doubt that had begun as a tiny seed had blossomed into a poisonous vine, threatening to consume his faith entirely.

Yohan, his spirit shrouded in doubt, became a ghost of his former self. The vibrant life he once led, filled with the rhythmic hum of his prayers and the comforting presence of his faith, had morphed into a desolate landscape of despair. His days, once meticulously structured around rituals and devotion, now stretched before him like an empty canvas, devoid of color and purpose.

One particularly bleak afternoon, the rain, a constant companion in his recent misery, hammered down relentlessly. Customers were scarce, and the silence in his shop hung heavy in the air. Yohan, slumped in his chair, stared out the rain-streaked window, his gaze vacant. The rhythmic tapping of the rain on the roof somehow mirrored the relentless beat of doubt echoing in his mind. Just then, the creak of the shop door announcing a new arrival startled him out of his reverie.

A tall, cloaked figure, shrouded in the dim light filtering through the rain-filled window, entered the shop. The air around him seemed to crackle with a strange energy, an unsettling aura that sent a shiver down Yohan's spine. The stranger, an elderly man with a kind face framed by a long, white beard, slowly approached Yohan, his eyes crinkled with a wisdom that seemed to pierce through the fog of doubt clouding Yohan's mind.

He extended a warm hand towards Yohan, his voice a husky whisper that somehow resonated with a strange familiarity. "Yohan," he greeted, his voice carrying an undercurrent of understanding. "May I have a seat?"

Yohan, momentarily stunned by the unexpected visitor, nodded in a daze. The stranger settled down on a stool across from him, his gaze holding Yohan's with an intensity that made him feel strangely exposed.

"A dark cloud seems to hang over you, Yohan," the stranger remarked gently, his words echoing Yohan's own internal turmoil. "Tell me, what troubles your heart?"

Yohan hesitated, unsure of this enigmatic visitor who seemed to possess an uncanny knowledge of his inner struggles. But something about the stranger's kindness and the sincerity in his voice made him loosen his grip on the dam holding back his emotions.

In a rush of words, fueled by months of bottled-up frustration and doubt, Yohan poured out his heart. He spoke of his unwavering faith, the meticulous rituals, and the seemingly futile prayers. He expressed his despair at the recent misfortunes; the dwindling business, Maya's illness, and the gnawing feeling that his devotion had been in vain.

As Yohan spoke, the air in the shop seemed to crackle with the raw emotion pouring out of him. The stranger listened patiently, his expression a canvas of empathy yet devoid of judgment. When Yohan finally finished his tirade, a heavy silence settled between them, broken only by the relentless drumming of the rain outside.

The stranger finally spoke, his voice a soothing balm on Yohan's troubled soul. "Yohan," he said, "faith is not about seeking blessings in exchange for blind devotion. It's about understanding the cycle of life, the interconnectedness of actions and consequences."

Yohan looked at the stranger, a flicker of hope battling the entrenched doubt clinging to his heart. "Are you saying my hardships are a result of past deeds?"

The stranger smiled gently. "Life is a tapestry woven from the threads of past actions, present choices, and unforeseen circumstances. True faith lies not in denying hardships but in navigating them with strength and resilience. Shani Bhagwan Ji's role is not to shield you from life's challenges but to guide you through them, to test your resolve and refine your character."

Yohan pondered the stranger's words. They echoed somewhere deep within him, resonating with a truth that transcended his current despair. Perhaps, he thought, faith wasn't a shield but a compass, a guiding force navigating him through the storms of life.

The stranger continued, "Doubt is a part of the journey, Yohan. It tests the strength of your convictions. But true faith emerges stronger from the fires of questioning. Your unwavering devotion has brought you here, to a point of introspection. Now, you have a choice. Will you allow doubt to consume you, or will you choose to rise above it, seeking answers and strengthening your faith?"

Yohan looked at the stranger, a newfound determination stirring within him. The darkness that had shrouded his heart began to recede, replaced by a faint ray of hope. This stranger, with his calm demeanor and insightful words, had planted a seed of understanding in his mind. Perhaps, Yohan thought, there was more to his faith than he had previously understood. Perhaps, the challenges he faced were not a punishment but a test, an opportunity to deepen his devotion on a more profound level.

The stranger's words hung in the air, a challenge intertwined with a promise. Yohan, his heart flickering with a nascent hope, sought answers. "What can I do to strengthen my faith? How can I navigate these challenges with a renewed sense of purpose?"

The stranger smiled enigmatically. "The answers you seek, Yohan, are not found in empty rituals or blind belief. They lie within yourself, in understanding the true essence of karma and devotion." He paused, letting his words sink in.

"Your journey begins with self-reflection," he continued. "Consider your past actions, the choices you made, both deliberate and inadvertent. Did you cause harm, even unintentionally, to others? Did you fail to uphold your duties or stray from the path of righteousness?"

Yohan's brow furrowed in concentration. He delved into the recesses of his memory, sifting through years of experiences. Though he considered himself an honest and fair man, a flicker of uncertainty flickered within. Perhaps, he hadn't always been as kind or compassionate as he believed. Maybe, in his pursuit of a successful business, he had taken shortcuts or engaged in practices that, while seemingly insignificant at the time, could have consequences.

The stranger observed Yohan's introspection with a knowing smile. "The seeds of our actions, Yohan, bear fruit both sweet and bitter. But remember, even darkness can be a fertile ground for growth."

"You mentioned karma," Yohan said, voicing his curiosity. "Is this hardship a result of my past deeds?"

"Karma," the stranger explained, "is the universal law of cause and effect. Every action, intentional or unintentional, carries a consequence. Your current difficulties might be the result of past actions, a balancing of the scales."

Yohan felt a knot form in his stomach. The idea that his hardships were a consequence of past errors brought a pang of guilt. Yet, a sense of clarity also dawned. Perhaps, understanding the cause was the first step towards rectification.

"So, what can I do now?" Yohan asked, his voice filled with a newfound determination. "How can I right the wrongs of the past?"

The stranger's eyes twinkled with a hint of amusement. "My role, Yohan, is not to provide easy answers," he replied. "But I can offer guidance. Seek out those you might have wronged, ask for forgiveness, and endeavor to right any imbalances. Focus on acts of kindness, contributing positively to the lives of others. As your actions align with the principles of righteousness, so will your life find its rightful balance."

Yohan digested the stranger's words, a sense of purpose rekindled within him. His faith, though shaken, wasn't completely shattered. It was a seed sown anew, a seed that required introspection, good deeds, and a deeper understanding of karma to truly flourish.

"Will you stay and guide me further?" Yohan pleaded, a flicker of anxiety welling up at the thought of the stranger leaving.

The stranger smiled warmly. "The answers you seek lie within you, Yohan. I have planted a seed, but it is you who must nurture it. Our paths may not cross again, but remember, Shani Bhagwan Ji's presence is always with you, guiding you through every step of your journey."

As he spoke, the rain outside began to subside, a sliver of sunlight peeking through the dark clouds. The stranger rose from his stool, his tall figure briefly casting a long shadow across the dimly lit shop.

"May your faith guide you through the darkness, Yohan," he said, his voice a gentle echo. With that, he turned, walked towards the rain-slicked street, and vanished into the swirling mist as quickly as he had appeared.

Yohan stood frozen, the stranger's parting words echoing in his mind. The shop, previously shrouded in gloom, now felt strangely lighter, as if a weight had been lifted. The stranger's visit, though brief, had ignited a spark within him, a renewed sense of purpose. His faith, though shaken, was no longer blind. It was a journey, a path of introspection, good deeds, and a deeper understanding of karma. Yohan looked out the window, the sun finally breaking through the clouds, casting a golden glow on the wet street. A new chapter in his life was about to begin, and he was ready to face it with his faith as his compass.

Chapter 2: Unveiling the Truth

Days turned into weeks after the enigmatic stranger's visit. Yohan, still grappling with the revelations about karma and faith, felt a renewed sense of purpose. The blind belief of his past had been replaced by a deeper understanding, a desire to actively shape his destiny through good deeds and self-reflection.

However, the question of how to move forward remained. The stranger's cryptic words about seeking answers within himself and righting past wrongs felt like a daunting task. Yohan yearned for guidance, a tangible starting point for his journey.

One morning, as Yohan knelt before the Shani Bhagwan Ji idol in the temple, a sense of clarity washed over him. He realized the answer might lie in revisiting his past, reflecting on his actions and interactions. Perhaps, the very experiences that brought him hardship held the key to understanding the karmic consequences he now faced.

Leaving the temple, Yohan felt a newfound determination in his stride. He returned to his shop, a plan slowly taking shape in his mind. The first step, he decided, was to revisit the places he had frequented in the past, the people he had interacted with regularly. Maybe, somewhere amongst those experiences, he would find the seeds of his current troubles.

He started with the local market, a bustling hive of activity where he had sourced materials for years. As he walked through the maze of stalls, memories flooded back. He recalled his haggling with vendors, sometimes pushing them for a lower price than they deserved. He had justified his actions, convinced he was simply being a shrewd businessman. Now, however, he saw them in a different light. His relentless pursuit of the best price might have caused unnecessary hardship for the vendors, a karmic imbalance that could explain his own current struggles.

Yohan approached one of the older vendors, a kind man named Gopal who had always treated him with respect despite their occasional disagreements. With a heavy heart, Yohan confessed his past behavior, apologizing for any anxiety or stress he might have caused. Gopal, a man of understanding, simply smiled and said, "We all make mistakes, Yohan. Let this be a learning experience for both of us."

Though a small gesture, the apology brought Yohan a sense of relief. It was a start, a small step towards rectifying the imbalances of his past. As he continued through the market, he interacted with other vendors, acknowledging his past behavior and seeking forgiveness. He vowed to treat them with more respect and fairness in the future, fostering a sense of mutual understanding.

Throughout the day, Yohan revisited other familiar places – his old neighborhood, the local tea stall he frequented, even the temple where he offered occasional donations. Everywhere he went, he searched for opportunities to set things right, to apologize for past mistakes, no matter how insignificant they might have seemed at the time.

The day was an emotional rollercoaster, filled with moments of regret, forgiveness, and a growing sense of purpose. By evening, Yohan felt a shift within himself. The burden of doubt that had weighed him down for weeks began to lift. Though challenges remained, he faced them with a newfound strength, his faith now rooted in understanding and action.

Days bled into weeks as Yohan continued his introspective journey. He meticulously revisited his past, unearthing memories he had long buried. One such memory, shrouded in a haze of regret, led him to the outskirts of Aayuthapura, a ramshackle settlement inhabited by the city's poorest residents.

Years ago, Yohan's father, a skilled carpenter, had been commissioned to build furniture for a wealthy merchant. The project required high-quality wood, a rare and expensive commodity. To cut costs, Yohan, then a young man eager to prove himself, convinced his father to use slightly lower-grade wood for hidden areas of the furniture. They completed the project, unaware that the merchant planned to resell it as a premium piece.

The consequences were swift and devastating. When the furniture began to deteriorate prematurely, the enraged merchant exposed Yohan's father's alleged deceit, tarnishing their reputation and causing a financial setback. The shame had driven Yohan's father to isolate himself, eventually contributing to his ill health and untimely demise.

Standing at the entrance of the settlement, a knot of guilt formed in Yohan's stomach. He remembered a specific family, the Kumars, who had been evicted from their home after failing to pay their debts to the very same merchant. The incident, a distant memory overshadowed by his grief, now took on a new significance.

He navigated the dusty lanes, the ramshackle houses a stark contrast to the bustling city center. He finally found the Kumars in a cramped one-room dwelling. The once-proud family was now a shell of its former self. The patriarch, a frail man with weary eyes, recognized Yohan.

Yohan, his voice thick with emotion, confessed his role in the events that led to their hardship. He apologized for the deceit and its devastating consequences. The family, initially stunned by the revelation, listened to his heartfelt apology. The patriarch, his face etched with a lifetime of hardship, spoke in a raspy voice.

"The past cannot be undone, young man," he said. "But your apology carries weight. It shows that you are striving to be a better person. Perhaps that is the true meaning of redemption."

Yohan left the settlement feeling a heavy weight lifted from his shoulders. Though the guilt of his past actions remained, the act of taking responsibility and seeking forgiveness offered a sense of closure. He realized that karma wasn't just about punishment; it was about learning and growth. He had faced a painful truth about his past, but in doing so, he had begun to understand the interconnectedness of actions and consequences.

As he walked back towards the city, the setting sun cast long shadows, painting the sky in hues of orange and red. The world seemed different, imbued with a deeper meaning. His journey towards self-discovery had just begun, but he felt a renewed sense of purpose. He was no longer a passive follower of rituals; he was an active participant in shaping his own destiny, one good deed and genuine apology at a time.

Weeks turned into months, and Yohan's life became a tapestry woven with introspection and acts of kindness. He continued his daily rituals at the temple, but his prayers now held a deeper meaning. They were expressions of gratitude for his blessings and a commitment to living a righteous life. His business, though still recovering from the monsoon's impact, began to show signs of improvement. Customers, drawn to his genuine nature and fair pricing, returned, and a sense of normalcy slowly seeped back into his life.

However, Yohan's newfound faith was about to be tested. One sweltering afternoon, as the city drowsed under the relentless summer sun, a commotion erupted outside his shop. A group of men, their faces contorted in anger, barged into his store. They were led by a burly man, his eyes glinting with malice.

Yohan recognized him instantly. It was Ashok, a notorious moneylender known for his ruthless tactics. Years ago, Yohan's father, facing a financial crisis due to the furniture fiasco, had borrowed a small sum from Ashok. The loan, with its exorbitant interest rates, had spiraled out of control, becoming a constant source of worry for the family.

Ashok, his voice dripping with venom, accused Yohan of refusing to repay the debt. He threatened to seize Yohan's shop and any remaining assets to settle the outstanding amount. Yohan, his heart pounding in his chest, tried to explain the situation, the deceit involved in the original loan, and his father's untimely demise.

Ashok scoffed at his explanation. "Lies!" he roared. "You are responsible for your father's debts. Pay up, or I'll take everything you have."

Yohan felt a surge of anger, a primal urge to defend himself. But then, he remembered the stranger's words: "True faith emerges stronger from the fires of questioning." This was his test, a chance to put his newfound understanding of karma into action.

He took a deep breath, calming himself. "I understand your anger, Ashok," he said, his voice surprisingly steady. "But threats won't solve this problem. Let's sit down and talk like reasonable men."

Ashok, surprised by Yohan's calm demeanor, reluctantly agreed. Over the next few hours, Yohan, armed with his knowledge of the original loan agreement and fueled by a newfound sense of assertiveness, negotiated with Ashok. He proposed a revised repayment plan, one that was fair and within his means.

The negotiation was tense, but Yohan held his ground. Finally, after much back-and-forth, Ashok, seeing the sincerity in Yohan's eyes and the strength of his resolve, agreed to the revised terms. He left the shop, his anger somewhat subdued, but with a promise to return for his monthly installments.

Yohan, drained but victorious, slumped back in his chair. He had faced his past, not with aggression, but with reason and compassion. He had upheld his principles, refusing to be bullied by a man who thrived on fear. This, he realized, was a significant step forward, a testament to the strength he derived from his evolving faith.

As the day drew to a close, a sense of peace settled over Yohan. The test had been grueling, but he had emerged stronger and more resolute. His faith, no longer a blind belief, was now a guiding force, empowering him to navigate the complexities of life with integrity and compassion. The path ahead might still hold challenges, but Yohan was no longer afraid. He was ready to face them head-on, one good deed and one act of courage at a time.

News of Yohan's encounter with Ashok spread through the marketplace like wildfire. People, who had witnessed his unwavering resolve and witnessed Ashok's concession, saw a newfound respect in Yohan. He became known not just for his craftsmanship, but also for his courage and his commitment to fairness.

One crisp morning, as Yohan opened his shop for the day, a majestic chariot pulled by magnificent black horses stopped outside. A hush fell over the bustling marketplace as a tall, imposing figure, clad in regal attire, emerged from the chariot. The figure, his head adorned with a shimmering crown, exuded an aura of power and wisdom. Yohan, his heart pounding in his chest, recognized him instantly from the countless depictions in temples and scriptures – Shani Bhagwan Ji himself.

The deity approached Yohan, his gaze radiating a gentle understanding. "Yohan," he boomed in a voice that resonated with the rhythm of the universe, "your journey of self-discovery has been closely observed."

Yohan fell to his knees, overwhelmed by the presence of the divine. Shani Bhagwan Ji extended a hand, helping him rise. "The trials you have faced," he continued, "were not punishments, but tests designed to strengthen your faith and character."

Yohan looked up at the deity, his eyes filled with gratitude. "I understand now, Shani Bhagwan Ji. My past actions had consequences, and my faith needed to be tested by fire."

Shani Bhagwan Ji nodded approvingly. "You have faced your past with honesty and sought forgiveness. You have navigated challenges with courage and compassion. Your actions have begun to right the imbalances created by your past deeds."

A wave of relief washed over Yohan. He felt the burden of doubt and despair finally lifting from his shoulders. Shani Bhagwan Ji continued, "Your faith, Yohan, is no longer based on blind devotion. It is a conscious choice, a commitment to living a righteous life. You have learned the true meaning of karma – the interconnectedness of actions and consequences."

Yohan felt a warmth spread through him, a validation of his introspection and good deeds. Shani Bhagwan Ji placed a hand on his shoulder. "Your journey continues, Yohan. But be assured, Shani Bhagwan Ji's presence is always with you, guiding you through every step."

With a final reassuring smile, Shani Bhagwan Ji turned and walked towards his chariot. The horses neighed as if in approval, and in a flash of light, the chariot and the deity vanished. The air crackled with a lingering energy, a tangible reminder of the divine encounter.

Yohan stood there, shaken yet empowered. His encounter with Shani Bhagwan Ji confirmed what he had learned through introspection and good deeds. Faith wasn't about seeking blessings in exchange for blind devotion; it was about navigating life's challenges with integrity, compassion, and a deep understanding of karma.

From that day forward, Yohan carried himself with a newfound confidence. He continued his business with honesty and fairness, treating everyone with respect. He actively participated in community events, offering his skills and resources to those in need. His journey of faith had evolved from blind belief to a conscious commitment to living a righteous life, inspiring others to walk the same path. The test of faith had revealed the true strength within him, a strength rooted in self-reflection, good deeds, and an understanding of the universe's interconnectedness. The path ahead was clear, and Yohan, his faith his guiding star, was ready to walk it with courage and compassion.

Chapter 3: Shadows in the Moonlight

Months flew by, a whirlwind of activity for Yohan. His dedication to fairness and ethical business practices resonated with his customers, attracting a loyal clientele. He thrived not just financially, but also in his sense of purpose. His faith, no longer a passive belief, was a guiding force in every interaction.

One sweltering summer evening, as Yohan settled down for a simple meal after closing his shop, a frantic pounding echoed on his door. He rose with a frown, his peaceful evening disrupted. Opening the door, he found a young woman, barely out of her teens, her face streaked with tears and fear.

"Please, you have to help me!" she gasped, her voice trembling with urgency.

Yohan ushered her into his dimly lit living area, offering her a seat and a glass of cool water. As she calmed down, she introduced herself as Maya, a young woman from a nearby village. She spoke of a growing darkness plaguing her village, a series of strange occurrences that had instilled fear in the hearts of the villagers.

"It started with nightmares," Maya explained, her voice barely a whisper. "Horrific visions that left everyone terrified. Now, shadows writhe on the walls at night, and whispers linger in the cool midnight air."

Yohan listened intently, his brow furrowed in concern. Though he didn't dismiss Maya's claims outright, a part of him wondered if her fear had amplified simple occurrences. Yet, the desperation in her eyes and the sincerity in her voice struck a chord within him.

"What have the village elders done?" he inquired, hoping to gain a better understanding.

Maya shook her head. "They are powerless against this unseen evil. They believe it's a curse, a vengeful spirit seeking retribution."

Yohan pondered the situation. His past experiences, particularly his encounter with the enigmatic stranger, had opened him to the possibility of unseen forces. Perhaps, this was a call to action, a chance to put his newfound faith to the test in a way he hadn't anticipated.

He looked at Maya, her fear palpable in the flickering lamplight. "I can't promise a solution," he said gently, "but I will come and see what I can do. Your village needs help, and I won't turn a blind eye to their plight."

A flicker of hope ignited in Maya's eyes. "Thank you," she breathed, a wave of relief washing over her. "You are our only hope."

Yohan, though unsure of what awaited him, felt a rising sense of determination. This was no longer about his own journey; it was about helping others, about using his faith and understanding to confront the unknown. Packing a few essentials and a lantern, Yohan and Maya set off towards the village under the watchful gaze of the moon, ready to face the shadows lurking in the night.

The journey to Maya's village was arduous. They walked for hours under the cool cloak of the night, the dusty path illuminated only by the pale glow of the moon and the flickering light from Yohan's lantern. Maya, her initial fear replaced by a quiet determination, recounted tales of the village's history, stories passed down through generations.

They reached the village nestled amidst a grove of ancient banyan trees as dawn began to paint the horizon with streaks of orange and pink. The village itself bore the marks of fear. Houses appeared abandoned, doors shut tight, and an unsettling silence hung heavy in the air. An old woman, her face etched with worry lines deeper than any Yohan had ever seen, approached them.

Recognizing Maya, the woman's eyes widened with relief. "You returned," she croaked, her voice raspy with age. "And you brought help?"

Maya introduced Yohan, explaining his willingness to assist them. The woman, who introduced herself as Amma, the village elder, led them to the center of the village, a clearing dominated by a weathered well.

"This is where the nightmares began," Amma explained, pointing towards the well. "One night, a bloodcurdling scream echoed from here. When we found our young Ramu unconscious, he spoke of a shadowy figure rising from the well, whispering promises of vengeance."

Yohan peered into the depths of the well. The darkness within seemed to writhe and pulsate, feeding his curiosity and trepidation. He remembered the stranger's words: "The answers you seek lie within yourself." This wasn't just about confronting an external evil; it was about understanding the source of the fear and finding a way to quell it.

As the sun climbed higher in the sky, casting its warm light upon the village, Yohan decided on a course of action. He questioned the villagers, meticulously recording their experiences. The nightmares, though terrifying, seemed to follow a similar theme – a shadowy figure emerging from the well, promising retribution.

Later that night, as the shadows stretched long and the moon cast an eerie glow, Yohan returned to the well, Maya and Amma by his side. He held the lantern high, its light barely penetrating the well's inky blackness. A cold wind seemed to emanate from the well, sending shivers down his spine.

Suddenly, a guttural voice echoed from the depths, its words laced with malice. "You dare disturb my slumber?" it boomed. "Prepare to face the consequences!"

Yohan, his heart pounding, took a deep breath. He knew fear wouldn't solve this problem. He raised his voice, his words clear and steady. "Who are you? Why are you tormenting this village?"

The voice chuckled, a sound that sent chills down their spines. "They have forgotten me," it rasped. "They have built their lives on stolen land, their prosperity stained with injustice."

Yohan exchanged a worried glance with Maya and Amma. There was a truth to the voice's words. The village had been built on land that was once disputed, a conflict shrouded in the mists of time.

"There is always a price to pay for injustice," the voice continued. "And now, they must face the consequences."

Yohan's mind raced. The entity's words resonated with his understanding of karma. The seemingly random terrorizing of the village was a consequence of an unresolved past injustice. He had a feeling that appeasing the entity wouldn't bring a permanent solution.

"There must be another way," Yohan declared, his voice firm despite the unsettling atmosphere. "A way to right the wrongs of the past and find peace."

The entity scoffed. "Peace? Those who sow discord cannot expect serenity."

Yohan ignored the entity's negativity. "Tell us about the stolen land," he said, his tone unwavering. "Who was wronged? What needs to be done?"

A tense silence followed. Then, the entity spoke again, its voice laced with a hint of surprise. "You seek true resolution? You are a curious one, mortal."

Yohan pressed on. "We can't move forward until we understand the past."

The entity, after a long, agonizing pause, began to narrate a tale of deceit and betrayal. Generations ago, the village elders had driven out a peaceful tribe from their ancestral land, promising them safe passage and fair compensation. However, those promises were broken, leaving the tribe displaced and filled with resentment.

The entity, a guardian spirit bound to the land, channeled the displaced tribe's anger and despair. Yohan listened intently, a sense of empathy welling up within him. This wasn't just about appeasing a vengeful spirit; it was about acknowledging past wrongs and seeking reconciliation.

"We can help find the descendants of the displaced tribe," Maya volunteered, her voice filled with conviction. "We can offer them a fair settlement, a chance to rebuild their lives."

A flicker of hope seemed to emanate from the well. The entity remained silent, but the air grew a little lighter, the oppressive feeling less intense.

Yohan turned to Amma, the village elder. "The path to healing won't be easy, Amma. It will require us to confront the truth and make amends."

Amma, her eyes filled with a newfound determination, nodded. "We have lived a lie for too long. It's time to set things right, even if it means sacrificing our own comfort."

A sense of accomplishment washed over Yohan. He hadn't banished the entity with a magical spell or defeated it with brute force. He had confronted the darkness with empathy, a desire for understanding, and a willingness to address the root cause of the problem.

"We will find the descendants," Yohan declared to the well, his voice echoing in the stillness of the night. "We will seek their forgiveness and offer them a path back to their rightful land. In doing so, we hope to find peace for both our village and the spirit that guards it."

As dawn approached, casting its golden light over the village, a sense of hope hung in the air. The darkness hadn't vanished entirely, but it had lost some of its power. The villagers, inspired by Yohan's courage and Maya's resolve, emerged from their homes, their eyes filled with a newfound determination to face their past and seek redemption.

Yohan knew that the journey wouldn't be easy. He wouldn't find the descendants in a day, nor would forgiveness be easily granted. Yet, for the first time since their arrival, a flicker of optimism danced in the eyes of Maya and Amma. The village, once shrouded in fear, now held the promise of a brighter future, built on truth, understanding, and the unwavering belief in the power of karma to restore balance.

The days following their encounter at the well were a whirlwind of activity. Yohan, Maya, and Amma, fueled by a newfound sense of purpose, delved into the village's history. Dusty archives yielded faded records and fragmented accounts, piecing together the tale of the displaced tribe. They discovered that the tribe, known as the Vanaras, had been skilled weavers renowned for their vibrant textiles.

With this information, Yohan and Maya embarked on a journey to track down the Vanara descendants. They traveled to neighboring villages, towns, and even distant cities, following any lead that might bring them closer to their goal. They met dead ends, encountered skepticism, and faced the harsh realities of a world where memories faded and communities dispersed.

However, their determination never wavered. Maya, fueled by a sense of responsibility for her village's past, and Yohan, guided by his unwavering faith, pressed on. Finally, after weeks of relentless pursuit, they found a small, isolated settlement nestled amidst rolling hills.

As they approached the settlement, a sense of familiarity washed over Yohan. The vibrant colors of the woven fabrics adorning the huts, the rhythmic click-clack of looms, and the warm smiles etched on the faces of the residents – it was an echo of the Vanara tribe's legacy.

They were met by an elder, a woman with eyes as deep and wise as the ancient well. Yohan, with a heavy heart, explained the purpose of their visit, narrating the tale of the stolen land and the fear gripping the village. He expressed his village's remorse and their genuine desire for reconciliation.

The elder listened patiently, her expression unreadable. When Yohan finished, a heavy silence descended. Finally, she spoke, her voice laced with a bittersweet sorrow.

"Generations have passed," she said. "The wounds of betrayal have festered, passed down through stories whispered by flickering lamplight. Forgiveness is not easily granted."

Despite the elder's words, Yohan felt a flicker of hope. The anger in her voice was tempered by a flicker of understanding. Maybe, just maybe, there was a chance for healing.

The elder revealed that the Vanaras, though displaced, had maintained their weaving traditions. Their textiles, imbued with the stories of their ancestors and the pain of their displacement, were prized throughout the land.

Yohan, inspired by this revelation, proposed a solution. He suggested a collaboration between the two villages. The Vanaras could provide training to the villagers in their weaving techniques, and in turn, the villagers could offer land and resources to help the Vanaras establish a thriving marketplace for their textiles.

The elder considered this proposal for a long moment. It was a path that offered not just reconciliation, but also a chance for both communities to prosper. Finally, she nodded in agreement.

The journey back to the village was filled with a newfound optimism. They carried not just a promise of reconciliation but also the seeds of a partnership that could bring prosperity to both communities.

As they approached the village, news of their success spread like wildfire. The villagers, who had been anxiously awaiting their return, erupted in cheers. The fear that had shrouded their lives for months began to lift, replaced by a sense of hope and anticipation.

A grand ceremony was held to mark the beginning of the collaboration. The Vanaras showcased their exquisite textiles, and the villagers, eager to learn the craft, listened intently. Laughter and shared stories filled the air, replacing the fear and suspicion of the past.

Yohan, standing amidst the joyous celebration, felt a deep sense of satisfaction. He had faced the darkness not with aggression or fear, but with empathy, understanding, and a commitment to finding a solution rooted in justice. His journey had taught him a valuable lesson – that true faith isn't about appeasing unseen forces, but about actively working towards a better future, one act of reconciliation at a time.

As the sun dipped below the horizon, casting an orange glow on the hopeful faces gathered, Yohan knew this was just the beginning. The path to true balance, he realized, was a continuous journey, a tapestry woven with threads of introspection, good deeds, and a relentless pursuit of understanding and justice.

Chapter 4: Echoes of
the Past

Months had passed since Yohan's encounter with the spirit guarding the well and the subsequent reconciliation with the Vanara tribe. The once-fearful village thrummed with a renewed sense of vitality. The collaboration with the Vanaras had blossomed, their vibrant textiles attracting merchants from far and wide. The villagers, adept learners, had begun incorporating the Vanara techniques into their own crafts, creating a unique blend of styles.

Yohan, his business thriving due to the increased prosperity in the village, felt a deep sense of fulfillment. His life, once focused on personal gain and blind faith, was now enriched by a sense of purpose. He actively participated in village activities, fostering a sense of community and helping to resolve minor disputes with his trademark fairness and calm demeanor.

One sweltering afternoon, as Yohan sat outside his shop, enjoying a cup of chai, a commotion erupted in the marketplace. A group of men, their faces contorted in anger, jostled with a lone figure draped in saffron robes. As Yohan approached, he recognized the saffron-clad figure – Swami Vivekananda, the revered spiritual leader who had recently arrived in the city.

The men, from a neighboring village known for its adherence to rigid traditions, accused Swami Vivekananda of heresy. They demanded his expulsion from the city, claiming his progressive views threatened their way of life.

Yohan, witnessing the unfolding scene, felt compelled to intervene. He pushed his way through the crowd, his voice calm but firm. "What's the meaning of this commotion?" he inquired.

One of the men, a burly fellow with a thick beard, glared at Yohan. "This heretic speaks against our customs! He mocks our faith!"

Swami Vivekananda, his demeanor calm despite the hostility around him, turned towards Yohan. "My friend," he spoke in a gentle voice, "I simply advocate for understanding and tolerance. All faiths have their place, and all paths can lead to enlightenment."

The men, however, remained unconvinced. The situation threatened to escalate, and Yohan knew he had to act. He remembered the words of the enigmatic stranger: "True faith embraces all paths, for they all lead to the same destination."

"Perhaps," he suggested, addressing the men, "we can all learn something from each other. Why not invite Swami Vivekananda to share his views in a peaceful setting? We can all listen and then decide for ourselves."

The men, taken aback by Yohan's suggestion, hesitated. Swami Vivekananda, however, offered a warm smile. "An excellent idea," he agreed. "Dialogue, not confrontation, is the path to understanding."

The crowd, sensing a possible resolution, murmured their agreement. Finally, the men from the neighboring village, though still skeptical, agreed to Yohan's proposal. It was decided that Swami Vivekananda would hold a discourse at the town hall the following evening, open to anyone who wished to attend.

Yohan, watching the crowd disperse, felt a surge of satisfaction. He had averted a conflict through reason and respect for differing viewpoints. As twilight painted the sky in hues of orange and purple, Yohan knew this was another test of his faith – a chance to foster understanding and bridge the gap between seemingly opposing beliefs.

The next evening, the town hall buzzed with anticipation. People from all walks of life, curious and intrigued, packed the hall to capacity. Swami Vivekananda, seated on a raised platform, radiated a serene calm amidst the bustling crowd. Yohan, along with Maya and Amma, stood at the back, observing the scene with a sense of hopeful anticipation.

As silence settled over the hall, Swami Vivekananda began his discourse. His voice, though soft, resonated with a quiet power. He spoke not of denouncing established traditions, but of the importance of open-mindedness and acceptance.

"Every religion," he explained, "is a beautiful tapestry, woven with threads of wisdom gathered across generations. Each path offers a unique perspective on the divine, a way to connect with the ultimate reality."

He spoke of the dangers of rigid adherence to dogma, the importance of questioning and seeking deeper understanding. He emphasized the universal values of compassion, love, and respect that formed the core of all faiths.

Swami Vivekananda's words resonated with the audience. Some, particularly the younger generation, nodded in agreement, their eyes gleaming with newfound understanding. Others, especially the older generation, listened intently, their faces etched with thoughtful contemplation.

Even the men from the neighboring village, who had initially arrived with hostility, seemed captivated by Swami Vivekananda's speech. His words, devoid of judgment or condescension, challenged their rigid beliefs without dismissing them entirely.

As the discourse concluded, a wave of applause filled the hall. People approached Swami Vivekananda, eager to ask questions and engage in further discussion. Yohan, observing the scene, felt a sense of accomplishment. His intervention had created a platform for dialogue, a space where diverse viewpoints could be expressed and considered with an open mind.

Later that evening, as Swami Vivekananda prepared to leave the city, he approached Yohan. "You have a kind heart and a wise soul, my friend," he said with a warm smile. "You understand that true faith thrives on open dialogue and the acceptance of differing paths."

Yohan humbled by Swami Vivekananda's praise, simply nodded. He had learned a valuable lesson that evening – that faith wasn't about blind acceptance of dogma, but about seeking truth through open-mindedness and fostering understanding amidst diverse beliefs.

The discourse had a profound impact on the community. While not everyone embraced Swami Vivekananda's progressive views entirely, a seed of doubt had been sown in their minds. The rigid adherence to tradition began to soften, replaced by a willingness to consider alternative perspectives.

Yohan, his faith strengthened by the challenges he had faced, continued on his journey. He knew the path wouldn't be easy, and there would be new challenges to overcome. But he was no longer afraid. He was armed with the unwavering belief that true faith wasn't a destination, but a continuous journey, a tapestry woven with threads of introspection, good deeds, and a relentless pursuit of understanding and tolerance.

News of the discourse and the shift in sentiment within the community spread like wildfire. It reached even the neighboring kingdom, ruled by the stern and conservative King Vikram. The king, a staunch traditionalist, viewed Swami Vivekananda's teachings as a threat to the established order. He saw a potential for unrest and rebellion if such liberal ideas were allowed to take root.

Driven by his anxieties, King Vikram summoned his most trusted advisor, a man known for his cunning and ruthlessness – Rajguru Kaal. The flickering lamplight danced on Kaal's face, highlighting the sharp gleam in his eyes as he listened to the king's concerns.

"This Swami Vivekananda," King Vikram thundered, his voice laced with anger, "speaks of tolerance and acceptance. He undermines the very foundation of our kingdom!"

Kaal stroked his beard thoughtfully. "Indeed, Your Majesty," he agreed, his voice a low rasp. "But perhaps we can turn this situation to our advantage."

He leaned closer to the king and whispered a plan, a devious scheme that would discredit Swami Vivekananda and reinforce the king's hold on his people's unwavering faith.

Meanwhile, unaware of the brewing storm, Yohan continued his work, striving to make a positive impact within his community. He organized workshops, inviting artisans from different regions to share their skills and techniques. The marketplace bustled with a vibrant mix of styles, fostering a sense of cultural exchange and mutual respect.

One day, a group of travelers arrived in the village. They hailed from the neighboring kingdom and carried a royal decree addressed to Yohan. The decree, signed by King Vikram himself, summoned Yohan to the royal court. It offered no explanation for the summons, leaving Yohan and the villagers baffled and a touch apprehensive.

Yohan knew that refusing a royal summons could be interpreted as defiance. Yet, a sense of unease gnawed at him. He decided to seek guidance from Maya and Amma.

Amma, her brow furrowed in worry, spoke first. "King Vikram is known for his strict adherence to tradition. This summons could be a trap."

Maya, her youthful optimism tempered by recent events, offered a different perspective. "Perhaps this is an opportunity to spread Swami Vivekananda's message of tolerance within the very walls of the king's court."

Yohan pondered their words. The potential risks were undeniable, but so was the opportunity to influence a powerful leader. He made a decision.

"I will go," he announced. "I will face whatever lies ahead, armed with my faith and the lessons I've learned."

The villagers, though worried, rallied around Yohan. They knew his journey to the king's court wouldn't be easy, but they also knew he wasn't one to shy away from a challenge.

With a heavy heart but a resolute spirit, Yohan packed a meager bag and prepared for his journey to the neighboring kingdom. He was aware of Rajguru Kaal's potential involvement and the unknown dangers that awaited him. However, he also carried a flicker of hope – the hope that his journey, born out of introspection and a commitment to understanding, might have an unexpected impact on the heart of a kingdom and its rigid ruler. As he embarked on this new challenge, Yohan knew this was just another chapter in his evolving faith, a testament to the enduring power of tolerance and the courage it takes to walk a path less traveled.

The journey to King Vikram's opulent palace was arduous. Yohan, accompanied by a single guard assigned by the village elder, traversed sun-baked plains and treacherous mountain passes. The long journey provided ample time for contemplation. He envisioned the austere court of King Vikram, a place where tradition reigned supreme. He pondered how he would navigate the court's rigid protocols and potential hostility, all while staying true to his newfound convictions.

Finally, after days on the road, the majestic spires of the royal palace pierced the horizon. Yohan, his heart pounding with a mix of anticipation and apprehension, entered the city gates. The bustling streets, teeming with the king's guards and adorned with symbols of unwavering faith, felt suffocating compared to the open and welcoming atmosphere of his village.

Upon arrival at the palace, Yohan was ushered into a grand hall, its opulence a stark contrast to his simple life. Rows of stern-faced courtiers flanked the entrance, their eyes scrutinizing the humble visitor. He bowed before a towering figure perched upon a jewel-encrusted throne – King Vikram himself.

The king's gaze was like a hawk's, sharp and piercing. "Yohan," he boomed, his voice echoing in the vast hall, "we have heard of your unorthodox ideas and your association with this so-called Swami Vivekananda."

Yohan stood tall, his voice betraying no fear. "Your Majesty," he began, "my faith is rooted in respect for all paths that lead to enlightenment."

A low murmur rippled through the court. King Vikram's expression darkened. "Enlightenment? You speak of heresy! You bring chaos to our kingdom with your tales of tolerance and acceptance."

Yohan remained undeterred. "True faith, Your Majesty, doesn't require rigid adherence to dogma. It embraces understanding and seeks truth through open dialogue."

The king scoffed. "Your words are hollow, Yohan. However, we have a task for you, a chance to prove your loyalty." He gestured towards Rajguru Kaal, who emerged from the shadows with a sly smile.

Kaal, his voice dripping with false sincerity, explained the king's "task." A sacred relic, a jewel believed to house a fragment of a divine being, had been stolen from the royal treasury. Yohan, known for his honesty and integrity, was to retrieve it. However, Kaal, with a veiled threat, made it clear that failure would be interpreted as collusion with the thieves.

Yohan, sensing a trap, knew this was no ordinary retrieval mission. It was a test, a ploy to discredit him and perhaps even brand him a thief if he failed to recover the nonexistent relic. With a deep breath, he accepted the task, determined to unravel the truth behind this elaborate scheme.

Thus began a treacherous investigation within the very walls of the palace. Yohan, with his keen eye for detail and his newfound understanding of the court's intricate politics, began his search. He observed the courtiers, their behavior, and their subtle interactions. He questioned servants, their voices filled with whispers and half-truths.

Days turned into weeks, and Yohan found no trace of the stolen relic. Yet, he stumbled upon something far more intriguing – evidence of Rajguru Kaal's duplicity. He discovered cryptic messages exchanged between Kaal and a shadowy figure outside the palace walls. The messages hinted at a staged theft, a ploy to eliminate any potential opposition to the king's absolute authority, possibly including Swami Vivekananda's growing influence.

Armed with this newfound knowledge, Yohan knew he had to act. He formulated a plan, a daring gamble that would expose Kaal's treachery and hopefully clear his own name. The stage was set for a confrontation, a battle not of swords, but of wit and unwavering faith.

Chapter 5: The Serpent's Coil

Yohan's heart pounded against his ribs like a trapped bird. He stood outside the King's private chambers, the ornately carved doors looming before him. In his hand, he clutched the intercepted messages – the irrefutable proof of Rajguru Kaal's devious plan. Exposing Kaal meant potential exile, even death, but staying silent could lead to the persecution of innocent people who dared to question the rigid traditions.

He took a deep breath, the scent of sandalwood incense heavy in the air. With a resolute hand, he knocked on the chamber doors. A tense silence followed, broken only by the rhythmic tap of his foot on the polished marble floor. Finally, the doors creaked open, revealing a young guard, his eyes wide with surprise.

"Yohan?" the guard stammered. "You seek an audience with the King?"

Yohan nodded curtly. "It's a matter of utmost urgency."

The guard, hesitant but respectful, relayed Yohan's request to the King. Moments later, a booming voice echoed from within, "Bring him in."

Yohan stepped into the chamber, his eyes adjusting to the dim light cast by flickering oil lamps. King Vikram sat on his throne, his face an unreadable mask. Rajguru Kaal stood beside him, a flicker of unease crossing his features as he saw Yohan enter.

Yohan bowed deeply. "Your Majesty," he began, his voice steady despite his racing heart. "I come bearing information regarding the missing relic."

A flicker of interest sparked in the King's eyes. "Speak," he commanded.

Yohan uncorked a small vial he had procured and held it aloft. Inside, a single, shimmering feather floated in a clear liquid. "This," he declared, "is a phoenix feather, a symbol of rebirth and renewal. It was found hidden within Rajguru Kaal's chambers."

Kaal's face contorted in fury. "Lies!" he roared. "This is a desperate attempt to frame me!"

Yohan remained calm. "Your Majesty," he continued, "I also possess intercepted messages that reveal Rajguru Kaal's communication with a known criminal outside the palace walls. These messages discuss a staged theft and a plot to silence anyone who challenges your authority."

He tossed a rolled-up scroll onto the table before the King. The King's expression hardened as he unfurled the scroll and scanned its contents. His gaze flickered between Yohan and Kaal, a storm brewing within him.

Yohan pressed on. "The relic, Your Majesty, was never stolen. It was a fabrication designed to incriminate anyone deemed a threat to Rajguru Kaal's influence."

A tense silence descended upon the chamber. The weight of Yohan's words hung heavy in the air. King Vikram's eyes narrowed as he studied both men before him. Kaal, his composure shattered, stammered a desperate plea for forgiveness, weaving a web of lies and accusations.

But the King had seen enough. With a thunderous voice, he slammed his fist on the armrest of his throne. "Enough!" he roared. "Rajguru Kaal, you stand accused of treason and deceit. You are hereby stripped of your position and your freedom. The guards will take you away."

Two guards materialized from the shadows and seized Kaal, who struggled in vain against their grip. As they dragged him from the chamber, his eyes met Yohan's with a venomous glare, a promise of revenge hanging heavy in the air.

The King turned to Yohan, a flicker of respect replacing the initial suspicion in his gaze. "You have shown courage and a keen mind, Yohan," he conceded. "You have exposed a viper who nestled at my side."

Yohan bowed again. "Thank you, Your Majesty. My only wish is that this kingdom may embrace tolerance and understanding instead of fear and suspicion."

King Vikram's response was not what Yohan anticipated. A long silence stretched between them, the only sound the crackling of the oil lamps. Finally, the King spoke, his voice laced with a hint of melancholy.

"Change," he said, "is a slow and arduous process, Yohan. My people are comfortable in their traditions. A sudden shift could lead to unrest."

Yohan understood the King's concerns. He countered, "But Your Majesty, can you truly maintain peace by stifling dissent? Perhaps a balance can be struck – one that respects tradition while allowing for open dialogue and exploration of different beliefs."

The King remained silent, contemplating Yohan's words. He glanced at the confiscated messages lying on the table, a symbol of the deception he had almost fallen victim to.

"Very well, Yohan," the King finally conceded. "You have earned a chance to present your ideas. I will arrange a discourse, similar to the one held by Swami Vivekananda, but within the confines of the palace for a select group of advisors and courtiers."

Yohan felt a surge of hope. This wasn't a complete victory, but it was a chance to plant the seeds of tolerance within the very heart of the kingdom.

The news of the upcoming discourse spread like wildfire. Whispers filled the palace corridors, some laced with curiosity, others with apprehension. Yohan, with the help of a learned scholar from the palace library, prepared his presentation. He wouldn't preach or condemn. He would share his own journey – his transformation from a follower of blind faith to someone who embraced understanding and respect for diverse beliefs.

The day of the discourse arrived. The atmosphere in the grand hall was tense. Nobles and advisors, adorned in their finest regalia, exchanged nervous glances. Yohan, standing behind a podium, took a deep breath.

He began by speaking not of religion, but of faith as a guiding light, a journey of self-discovery. He spoke of the importance of questioning, of seeking knowledge from different sources. He emphasized the beauty in the tapestry woven with threads of various beliefs, each leading to the same ultimate truth.

As Yohan spoke, the initial unease gradually melted away. The courtiers, accustomed to pronouncements from the King, were intrigued by his personal narrative and his message of tolerance. Some even nodded in agreement, their faces reflecting a shift in perspective.

By the end of the discourse, a sense of thoughtful silence filled the hall. Yohan didn't expect immediate conversion, but he saw a flicker of understanding in the eyes of some. One advisor, a man renowned for his staunch traditionalism, approached Yohan after the discourse.

"Your words were... thought-provoking," he admitted, a hint of surprise in his voice. "Perhaps there is truth to be found in exploring other perspectives."

This small victory, a single seed of tolerance planted in fertile ground, filled Yohan with a newfound sense of purpose. He had faced a powerful king and a cunning advisor, not with violence or threats, but with the unwavering conviction of his faith and a message of understanding.

As he left the palace walls and stepped out into the bustling city, Yohan knew this was just another chapter in his ongoing journey. He would continue to advocate for tolerance, knowing that change, like faith, is a tapestry woven with threads of courage, conviction, and the enduring hope for a more peaceful and understanding world.

News of Yohan's successful discourse within the palace walls rippled outwards like a pebble tossed into a still pond. Whispers of "tolerance" and "open dialogue" reached the ears of the common people, sparking curiosity and cautious optimism.

Meanwhile, within the palace, a subtle shift began to take place. The King, though still a firm believer in tradition, found himself contemplating Yohan's words. The fear-mongering tactics of Rajguru Kaal now seemed hollow compared to the message of understanding. He began to loosen his grip on absolute control, allowing for more open discussions within the court.

Yohan, his reputation as a champion of tolerance preceding him, received numerous invitations to speak at various gatherings throughout the kingdom. He addressed merchants in bustling marketplaces, scholars in ancient libraries, and even skeptical farmers tilling their land. He spoke not as a preacher, but as a storyteller, sharing his personal transformation and highlighting the benefits of fostering a spirit of understanding.

His message resonated with many. Some, particularly the younger generation, embraced the idea of open dialogue and exploration. Others, more cautious, were willing to at least consider the possibility of peaceful coexistence with differing beliefs. Even some staunch traditionalists, initially resistant to change, found themselves softening their views in the face of Yohan's sincerity and the growing popularity of his message.

However, the seeds of tolerance weren't sown without resistance. Rajguru Kaal, now imprisoned within the palace dungeon, plotted his revenge. He smuggled messages out, rallying his loyal followers – a group of religious fanatics who thrived on fear and division.

One night, while Yohan was addressing a gathering in a remote village, a group of cloaked figures emerged from the shadows. They hurled accusations of heresy and incited chaos among the crowd. Yohan, surrounded by the mob, remained calm. He tried to reason with them, but his words were drowned out by their angry shouts.

Suddenly, a familiar voice rose above the din. Maya, along with a group of villagers from Yohan's village, had arrived. They stood alongside Yohan, forming a human shield against the angry mob. They didn't fight back, but instead, countered the accusations with messages of peace and understanding.

The unexpected display of unity had a profound impact. Shamefaced, some members of the mob began to back down. Others, their anger subsiding, started listening to the message of tolerance.

Seeing his attempt to incite violence foiled, the leader of the mob, a man with a cruel glint in his eyes, lunged towards Yohan. However, before he could reach him, a figure emerged from the darkness. It was a former palace guard, one who had admired Yohan's courage during his trial before the King. He tackled the mob leader, disarming him before the guards could intervene.

The incident solidified Yohan's place as a symbol of tolerance and understanding. News of his courage and the villagers' unwavering support spread far and wide. The King, upon learning of the attack, ordered a swift investigation, uncovering Rajguru Kaal's involvement. Kaal's remaining followers were apprehended, their attempts to sow discord thwarted.

Years passed, and the kingdom witnessed a gradual yet significant shift. Open dialogue became more commonplace. Religious festivals, once held separately, were celebrated together, fostering a spirit of community and understanding. While some traditionalists held onto their rigid beliefs, they no longer viewed those with differing faiths as enemies but as neighbors.

Yohan, his hair now streaked with grey, continued his work. He had become a revered figure, a living testament to the power of faith and the importance of tolerance. He had faced challenges and dangers, but his journey had reaffirmed his belief – that true faith isn't about blind acceptance, but about fostering understanding and building bridges across divides, one thread of tolerance at a time.

As he sat by his window, watching the sun set over the peaceful village, Yohan knew his work was far from over. The world was a vast tapestry woven with diverse beliefs, and there would always be challenges. But he also knew that the seeds of tolerance he had planted had taken root, leaving behind a legacy of hope – a promise of a world where faith could guide humanity towards a brighter, more peaceful future.

Yohan's influence wasn't confined to the kingdom he had helped transform. Whispers of his journey and the blossoming spirit of tolerance within the kingdom's walls reached far beyond its borders. Merchants, scholars, and travelers carried his message like precious seeds, planting them in fertile ground across the land.

In a distant kingdom known for its fierce adherence to a single deity, a young scholar named Amara stumbled upon a weathered scroll depicting a vibrant tapestry. It showcased various symbols from different faiths, woven together in a harmonious blend. Intrigued, she delved deeper, discovering tales of Yohan's journey and the kingdom's transformation.

Amara, yearning for a world beyond rigid dogma, felt a spark ignite within her. Inspired by Yohan's message, she began sharing the story of the tapestry and the importance of understanding with her fellow scholars. Initially met with skepticism, her words resonated with a growing number of young minds.

Meanwhile, in a bustling trade city on the opposite side of the continent, a young merchant named Khalil overheard tales of a kingdom where diverse beliefs coexisted peacefully. Curiosity gnawed at him, for his own city was riddled with religious tension. He longed for a world where merchants like him could trade freely without fear of persecution due to their faith.

Driven by this newfound hope, Khalil embarked on a journey to the transformed kingdom. He witnessed firsthand the tolerance Yohan had championed and returned home brimming with inspiration. He organized gatherings, bringing together merchants from different faiths to share stories and forge connections.

These ripples of change, though seemingly insignificant at first, began to spread outwards, creating a gentle wave that threatened to erode the rigid walls of intolerance. Religious leaders, initially resistant to these new ideas, found themselves challenged to defend their rigid doctrines in the face of growing public discourse.

News of these developments eventually reached Yohan, now an elder statesman in his own kingdom. A sense of profound satisfaction washed over him. His journey, which began with a simple quest for personal truth, had blossomed into a movement for understanding that transcended borders and challenged the very foundations of religious extremism.

One sunny afternoon, Yohan received a visit from an unexpected guest – Amara, the young scholar from the distant kingdom. She had made a perilous journey to seek his guidance and share the progress she had made in fostering a spirit of tolerance in her own land.

Yohan listened intently, a proud smile gracing his wrinkled face. "You see, Amara," he said with a twinkle in his eye, "faith, like a tapestry, thrives on the inclusion of diverse threads. It is in the blending of perspectives that we find the true beauty and strength of our beliefs."

Amara nodded, her eyes gleaming with newfound determination. "Your journey, Yohan, has inspired a generation to challenge the status quo and embrace the power of understanding. We may be weaving different tapestries, but ultimately, we are all striving for the same – a world where faith brings us together, not divides us."

As they sat under the shade of a sprawling banyan tree, sharing stories and dreams, Yohan knew this was just the beginning. The tapestry of tolerance, once a single thread in his life, had become a vast canvas, woven with the hopes and aspirations of countless individuals across the land. And he, the man who had once sought blind faith, now stood as a symbol of the enduring power of understanding and the unwavering belief in a brighter future for all.

About the Author

Mrigendra Bharti, born on June 29, 2004, in South Delhi, India, is a multifaceted individual recognized as the owner of Mrigendra Bharti Group InfoTech India Co. Pvt Ltd. Beyond his entrepreneurial endeavors, he is a distinguished music producer, director, and a budding writer.

Embarking on his professional journey at a young age, Mrigendra Bharti's visionary leadership has led to the establishment of several successful ventures, including Croma Music Series Entertainment, Sellbrochure, Fauget Innovative, and more.

What sets Mrigendra apart is his early initiation into the world of business. His foray into the unknown realms of entrepreneurship began during his 10th-grade years, where he delved into the music industry. This initial venture laid the foundation for subsequent achievements, showcasing his dedication and resilience.

Having honed his skills in music, Mrigendra Bharti not only demonstrated significant growth in his craft but also expanded his professional network. His passion extends beyond music, encompassing app and website development, as well as graphic design.

Fueled by his creative aspirations, Mrigendra established the Mrigendra Bharti Group, a company specializing in website and app development. Currently, he collaborates with a dedicated team, collectively working on ambitious projects that promise innovation and excellence.

Mrigendra's journey serves as an inspiration, particularly for today's students, highlighting the potential of youthful determination and the ability to transform innovative ideas into successful businesses. As he continues to make strides in various domains, Mrigendra Bharti remains a dynamic force, contributing vibrancy to the realms of business, music, and technology.

Read more at https://www.imwriter-mrigendra.rf.gd.